THERE WAS AN OLD LADY WHO SWALLOWED FLY GUY

Tedd Arnold

CARTWHEEL BOOKS
An Imprint of Scholastic Inc.

For Marissa, Benjamin, Ethan,
Gary, and Amy — of course!
—T. A.

Copyright © 2007 by Tedd Arnold.

All rights reserved. Published by Scholastic Inc. *Publishers since 1920.*
SCHOLASTIC, CARTWHEEL BOOKS, and associated logos are
trademarks and/or registered trademarks of Scholastic Inc.

The publisher does not have any control over and does not assume any responsibility for
author or third-party websites or their content.

ISBN 978-0-545-84871-8
10 9 8 7 6 5 4 3 2 1   15 16 17 18 19
Printed in the U.S.A.   40
This edition first printing, January 2015

A young boy named Buzz
had a pet fly.
No one knows why
he had a pet fly.
Buzz named him Fly Guy.

<u>Chapter 1</u>

One day Buzz went
to visit his grandma.
Fly Guy went, too.

Grandma was happy
to see Buzz.
She ran to hug him.

"Hi, Grandma!" said Buzz.
"I want you to meet my pet..."

Grandma said—

GLURK!

and she swallowed Fly Guy.

Buzz didn't know why
she swallowed Fly Guy.

Chapter 2

Fly Guy went down
a deep dark hole.

At the bottom of the hole,
he came to a wet place.

He looked around for a while.
Then he wanted to leave.

He started up the hole.

Just then, Grandma
swallowed a spider
to catch Fly Guy.

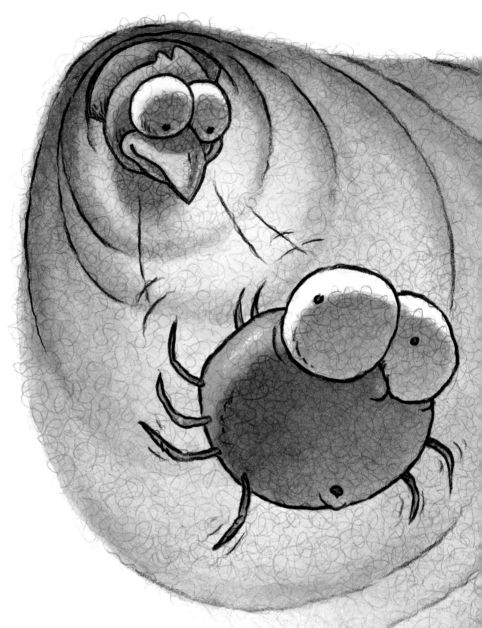

She swallowed a bird
to catch the spider.

She swallowed a cat
to catch the bird.

She swallowed a dog
to catch the cat.

She swallowed a goat
to catch the dog.

She swallowed a cow
to catch the goat.

Chapter 3

Grandma was about to
swallow a horse
to catch the cow.

Fly Guy cried,  **BUZZ!**

"I'm up here!" yelled Buzz.

Out came Fly Guy.

Out came the spider,
the bird, the cat, the dog,
the goat, and the cow.

And everyone lived
happily ever after,
of course!